Evelina Daciūtė
Aušra Kiudulaitė

THE FOX ON THE SWING

Thames & Hudson

ONCE UPON A TIME, THERE WAS A BOY NAMED PAUL.

WAIT,
THAT'S NOT
QUITE RIGHT.

THIS STORY BEGINS
IN A DIFFERENT WAY...

NEEE NAH
NEEE NAH
13
FANCY
FOOD
TRUCK
TAXI
BIG TRUNKS WELCOME
WONDER WEDDING
LIMOUSINE SERVICE
BUSY BUS

IN A BIG CITY,
THERE WAS A
PRETTY PARK.
ON THE EDGE
OF THE PARK,
THERE WAS A
VERY
TALL
TREE,

WHICH HAD BEEN
GROWING THERE FOR
A VERY LONG TIME.

1
PARK
STREET

THE TREE WAS SPECIAL NOT ONLY BECAUSE
IT WAS VERY OLD AND VERY TALL,
BUT BECAUSE PEOPLE LIVED INSIDE IT:

A BOY NAMED PAUL,
HIS MOTHER
AND HIS FATHER.

THEY WERE A FAIRLY NORMAL FAMILY,
APART FROM THE FACT THAT
THEY LIVED IN A
TREE.

EVERY MORNING, PAUL'S FATHER CLIMBED A LADDER TO THE TOP OF THE TREE.
THERE WAS A SMALL HELICOPTER PAD UP THERE AND AN
ORANGE HELICOPTER.

PAUL'S FATHER WOULD GET INTO THE HELICOPTER AND FLY AWAY OUT OF SIGHT. IT WAS HIS JOB TO TAKE PEOPLE AND THINGS

FROM ONE PLACE TO ANOTHER.

FLIES

THINGS

PEOPLE

PAUL'S MOTHER

WORKED AT HOME, MAKING THINGS OUT OF CLAY. SHE MADE VASES, BOWLS AND POTS.

MOST OF THEM WERE ORANGE.

WHEN SHE'D MADE SO

SO MANY POTS

THAT THERE WAS NO ROOM
TO WALK ACROSS THE FLOOR,
PAUL'S FATHER WOULD PILE
ALL OF HER POTTERY INTO HIS
HELICOPTER AND TAKE IT TO
A SHOP IN THE CITY WHERE
IT WOULD BE SOLD.

EVERY AFTERNOON, PAUL'S MOTHER
ASKED HIM TO RUN DOWN TO THE BAKERY
TO BUY FRESH BREAD ROLLS.

"WHEN YOUR DAD COMES HOME,
WE'LL SIT DOWN TOGETHER AND
DRINK TEA AND EAT THE ROLLS.
THEY'LL BE SO DELICIOUS!"

THEN SHE WOULD GIVE PAUL
SOME MONEY AND A BAG
TO CARRY THE ROLLS.

WHAT PAUL LIKED BEST WAS
TO TAKE THE SHORTEST ROUTE
TO THE BAKERY, AND THE LONG WAY HOME.

WALKING THE SAME WAY
TWICE WAS A LITTLE BIT
BORING, AFTER ALL.

ON HIS WAY TO THE BAKERY, HE SAW PARENTS
WITH BABIES, RUNNERS, CYCLISTS, DOG WALKERS
AND KIDS RIDING SCOOTERS AND SKATEBOARDS.

WHEN HE REACHED THE EDGE OF THE PARK, HE COULD FIND THE BAKERY WITH HIS EYES CLOSED. IN FACT, HE OFTEN TRIED TO DO EXACTLY THAT.

HE WOULD SHUT HIS EYES

AND LET THE WONDERFUL SMELL LEAD HIM TO THE BAKERY. SOMETIMES IT WORKED, BUT SOMETIMES HE WOULD TRIP OVER A STONE OR BUMP INTO SOMEONE ELSE. NOBODY LIKED THAT.

ONCE HE ARRIVED AT THE BAKERY, PAUL WOULD GIVE HIS MONEY TO THE BAKER, MAGGIE, WHO MADE ALL THE BREAD AND CAKES HERSELF.

PAUL WOULD ASK FOR THREE FRESH ROLLS

AND MAGGIE WOULD PUT THEM IN A PAPER BAG FOR HIM. THEN PAUL WOULD SET OFF FOR HOME.

PAUL ALWAYS KEPT HIS EYES
WIDE OPEN AS HE WALKED HOME.

HE DIDN'T WANT
TO MISS A THING.

HE SAW STRANGELY SHAPED STONES,
FASCINATING TWISTED ROOTS, FANCY BIRDS
THAT HAD ESCAPED FROM THE ZOO, AND
PUDDLES THAT GLISTENED ON THE GROUND.

UT THE THING THAT PAUL LIKED MOST OF ALL WAS THE OLD SWING IN THE PARK.

NOT TO SWING ON HIMSELF, BUT BECAUSE THERE WAS A FOX WHO LIKED TO CURL UP AND SLEEP ON THE SEAT OF THE SWING.

PAUL DIDN'T SEE HER THERE EVERY DAY, MAYBE ABOUT ONCE A WEEK.

ONE DAY, PAUL SAW SOMETHING HE COULD HARDLY BELIEVE. THE FOX WAS ACTUALLY SWINGING ON THE SWING. THE FOX SAW PAUL AND JUST KEPT ON SWINGING.

THEN SHE STOPPED, SNIFFED AT THE AIR, LOOKED PAUL IN THE EYE AND SAID:

"BEING GENEROUS IS LIKE AN OCEAN. WOULD YOU LIKE TO BE A DROP IN THAT OCEAN?"

PAUL DIDN'T UNDERSTAND, BUT HE NODDED ANYWAY.

"THEN GIVE ME ONE OF YOUR ROLLS," THE FOX SAID.

CARING MEANS SHARING

PAUL DIDN'T REALLY WANT TO SHARE THE ROLLS WITH THE FOX. THERE WERE ONLY THREE ROLLS, ONE FOR HIMSELF, HIS MOTHER AND HIS FATHER. HOWEVER, AFTER FROWNING JUST A LITTLE, HE TOOK OUT HIS OWN ROLL AND GAVE IT TO THE FOX. AFTER THAT, WHENEVER HE MET THE FOX, HE GAVE HER HIS ROLL.

ON THOSE DAYS, PAUL'S PARENTS DID NOT QUITE BELIEVE HIS STORY ABOUT THE FOX AND WHY THE THIRD ROLL HAD DISAPPEARED. BUT WHEN THEY SAT DOWN FOR TEA, THEY WOULD BREAK OFF PIECES OF THEIR OWN ROLLS AND GIVE THEM TO PAUL.

"HAVING A FOX AS YOUR FRIEND IS THE SAME AS SWINGING ON A SWING," PAUL SAID AS HE ATE. "THERE ARE UPS AND DOWNS. ONE DAY IT MIGHT BE FUN. THE NEXT DAY IT MIGHT NOT BE SO FUN."

SOME DAYS HE FOUND THE FOX IN A BAD MOOD.
LOST! ONE GOOD MOOD. IF FOUND, PLEASE RETURN TO FOX
AT LEAST I'VE STILL GOT WIFI...

"I'M DOWN IN THE DUMPS," THE FOX MIGHT SAY.
SOMETIMES SHE ADDED, "I HAVE A BAD CASE
OF THE BLUES." AND WHEN A FOX HAS
THE BLUES, THERE'S NOT MUCH YOU CAN
DO TO MAKE IT BRIGHT AND ORANGE AGAIN.

THE FOX WOULD TELL PAUL ALL SORTS OF STORIES THAT SHE HAD HEARD FROM HER GRANDMOTHER, WHO WAS A VERY WISE OLD FOX. PAUL DID NOT ALWAYS UNDERSTAND THE STORIES. THEY WERE A LITTLE BIT STRANGE.

"ARE YOU CALLING MY STORIES STRANGE?"

ASKED THE FOX IN A TEMPER.

"MY STORIES ARE PERFECTLY FINE. IT MUST BE YOU THAT'S STRANGE."

UP ABOVE

WHERE THE RAIN FALLS DOWN

PAUL TOLD THE FOX STORIES ABOUT HIS OWN LIFE. OFTEN HE ASKED HER FOR ADVICE.

"MY GRANDFATHER WAS A WISE OLD FOX,"

THE FOX WOULD SAY. "HE TOLD ME THAT EVERYTHING DEPENDS ON YOUR POINT OF VIEW. THINGS CAN CHANGE, DEPENDING ON WHETHER YOU LOOK AT THEM FROM UP ABOVE OR DOWN BELOW, FROM THE LEFT OR FROM THE RIGHT. SO ASK ME AGAIN WHEN YOU'VE LOOKED AT THE PROBLEM FROM ALL SIDES."

LEFT

RIGHT

OWN BELOW

ONE DAY, WHEN THE FOX
WAS IN A VERY GOOD MOOD, SHE SAID,
"THE BEST THING TO DO IS JUST
KEEP ON SWINGING."

THEN SHE EXPLAINED THAT
THE HAPPIEST THINGS IN THE WORLD ARE
ORANGE.

"HAPPINESS IS A FOX ON A SWING AND A BIG ORANGE ORANGE!" SHE YELLED AS THE SWING CARRIED HER HIGH INTO THE SKY. "HAPPINESS IS CARROT CAKE, GOLDFISH, MARMALADE, AND TREES IN AUTUMN!"

MEOW

THEN SHE LET PAUL TAKE A TURN ON THE SWING.

AS HE FLEW THROUGH THE AIR, PAUL CALLED OUT: "HAPPINESS IS MY MOTHER'S POTS AND MY DAD'S HELICOPTER! HAPPINESS IS AN ORANGE BASKETBALL AND MAGGIE'S GINGER CAT!

BUT MOST OF ALL,

HAPPINESS IS A FOX!"

"WILL I ALWAYS
FIND YOU
HERE?"
PAUL ASKED.

"OF COURSE NOT,"
THE FOX REPLIED.
"WHEN I NEED TO
BE SOMEWHERE ELSE,
THAT'S WHERE
I'LL GO."

"BUT WHAT ABOUT ME?"

PAUL ASKED SADLY.

THE FOX THOUGHT ABOUT THAT FOR A MOMENT.

"FOR A WHILE, I THINK YOU'LL WALK THIS WAY AND STILL EXPECT TO FIND ME HERE. THEN YOU'LL STOP COMING THIS WAY, SO YOU DON'T HAVE TO SEE THIS PLACE AND THIS SWING ANY MORE. BUT SOONER OR LATER, SOMEONE WILL COME ALONG TO TAKE MY PLACE."

AFTER THIS CONVERSATION, THINGS WERE NEVER THE SAME AGAIN. PAUL FELT UNEASY AS HE WALKED THE LONG WAY HOME. IF THE FOX WASN'T THERE, HE WORRIED THAT HE'D NEVER SEE HER AGAIN. IF SHE WAS THERE, HE FELT HAPPIER THAN HE'D EVER FELT BEFORE.

VERY GOOD NEWS

ONE DAY, PAUL'S FATHER CAME HOME FROM WORK MUCH HAPPIER THAN USUAL. HE KISSED PAUL'S MOTHER AND LIFTED PAUL HIGH UP INTO THE AIR. HE TOLD THEM THAT SOON THEY WOULD BE MOVING TO AN EVEN BIGGER CITY, WHERE THEY WOULD LIVE IN AN EVEN TALLER TREE IN AN EVEN BIGGER PARK. AND HE WOULD FLY AN

EVEN BIGGER

HELICOPTER.

"EVERYTHING WILL BE SO MUCH BETTER THAN BEFORE!" PAUL'S FATHER SAID.

"BUT WHAT IF WE'RE HAPPY ENOUGH ALREADY?" PAUL ASKED. HE REALLY DIDN'T WANT TO LIVE ANYWHERE ELSE.

"THERE'S NO SUCH THING AS BEING HAPPY ENOUGH," HIS FATHER SAID.

"THINGS CAN ALWAYS GET BETTER."

THE NEXT TIME THEY MET,
PAUL AND THE FOX LOOKED UP AT THE STARS TOGETHER.
THEN PAUL TOLD THE FOX THAT HE WAS
GOING TO MOVE AWAY.

"SO THIS IS HOW IT HAPPENS. YOU'RE GOING TO
DISAPPEAR AND I WILL STAY HERE," THE FOX SAID.

"I'M NOT DISAPPEARING. THEY'RE MAKING ME MOVE.
IT'S NOT THE SAME THING," PAUL CRIED.
"I DON'T WANT TO LEAVE. I WANT TO STAY HERE.
YOU'RE MY BEST FRIEND."

"MY FATHER, WHO WAS A VERY WISE FOX,
ALWAYS SAID THAT IT TAKES TIME TO KNOW
WHEN SOMETHING IS GOOD," THE FOX SAID TO PAUL.

"IMAGINE A CAKE WITH CREAM INSIDE. YOU MIGHT
NOT BITE INTO THE CREAM RIGHT AWAY, BUT ONLY
GET TO IT AFTER A FEW BITES. IF YOU KEEP EATING,
THE CAKE WILL TASTE BETTER AND BETTER."

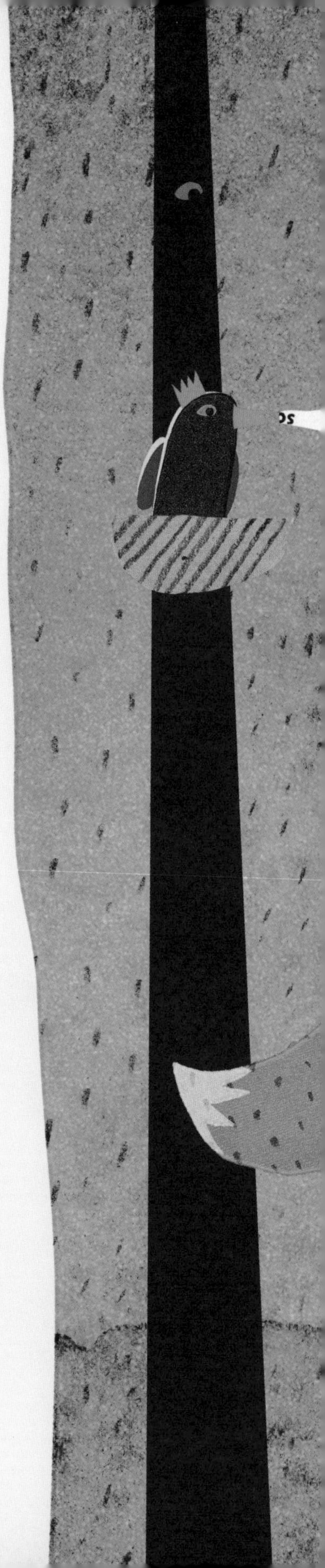

THE NEW BOOT
THE BOX ON WHEELS
THE BIG KEY
THE WISE OLD FOX
THE SWISS ROLL
THE JAR OF JAM
THE ELEPHANT
THE STAR CAT
THE HAPPY BIRD
THE CARROT
OF THE NORTH
THE GOLDFISH
THE BASKETBALL
THE GIANT PEACH
THE SECOND
SWISS ROLL
THE RUNAWAY KITE

DAISY'S DAIRY
FRESH MILK AND CREAM
TAXI
HALF-PRICE FOR HAT WEARERS
SPEEDY SNAIL
MAIL
VERY BUSY BUS

A WEEK LATER, PAUL AND HIS PARENTS CLIMBED INTO THE BIGGER HELICOPTER AND FLEW TO THE BIGGER PARK IN THE BIGGER CITY, TO THEIR BIGGER HOME IN THE TALLER TREE. DAYS WENT BY, BUT PAUL DID NOT FEEL ANY BETTER, ONLY WORSE.

PAUL FELT ANGRY. "YOU PROMISED EVERYTHING WOULD BE BETTER HERE," HE SAID TO HIS FATHER.

"YOU NEED TO GIVE IT SOME TIME," PAUL'S MOTHER SAID. "JUST WAIT A LITTLE LONGER, AND THINGS WILL GET BETTER."

"TRY TO BE PATIENT," HIS FATHER ADDED. "REMEMBER, GOOD THINGS COME TO THOSE WHO WAIT."

JUST LIKE BEFORE, PAUL WALKED TO THE BAKERY EVERY DAY.

THE NEW BAKERY WAS BIGGER THAN THE OLD ONE AND TWO BAKERS WORKED THERE. THEIR NAMES WERE EMILY AND ROSE. ONE OF THEM WOULD PUT THREE FRESH ROLLS INTO A PAPER BAG AND PAUL WOULD WALK HOME THE SAME WAY HE HAD COME.

ONE DAY, ON HIS WAY HOME FROM THE BAKERY, PAUL SAW A PATH WINDING THROUGH THE WOODS. HE HADN'T NOTICED IT BEFORE. FEELING CURIOUS, HE HEADED DOWN THE PATH.

AS HE WALKED, HE NOTICED STRANGELY SHAPED STONES AND FASCINATING TWISTED ROOTS. HE SAW FANCY BIRDS THAT LOOKED AS THOUGH THEY HAD ESCAPED FROM THE ZOO, AND PUDDLES THAT GLISTENED ON THE GROUND.

PAUL BEGAN TO RUN ALONG THE PATH, JUMPING IN THE AIR FOR JOY. HE WAS HAVING SO MUCH FUN! THEN SUDDENLY, IN THE DISTANCE, HE SAW A SWING. THE SWING WAS FLYING BACK AND FORTH THROUGH THE AIR. AND THERE ON THE SWING WAS THE ORANGE FOX.

trees
trees trees
trees
trees
trees trees
trees

"FOX!"

PAUL CALLED OUT.

"HOW DID YOU GET HERE?"

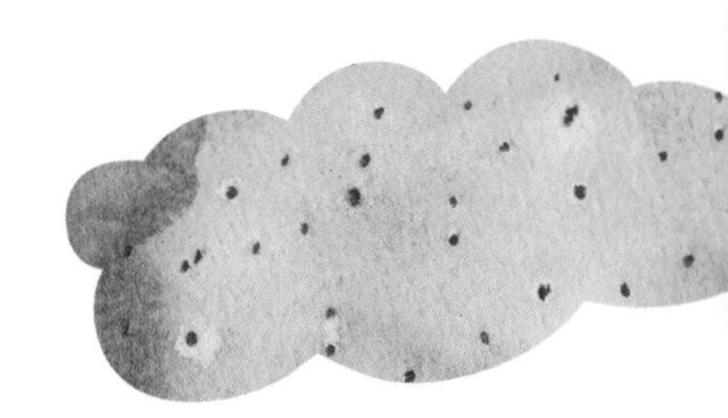

"I TOLD YOU," THE FOX ANSWERED.

"WHEN I NEED TO BE SOMEWHERE ELSE,

THAT'S WHERE I GO."

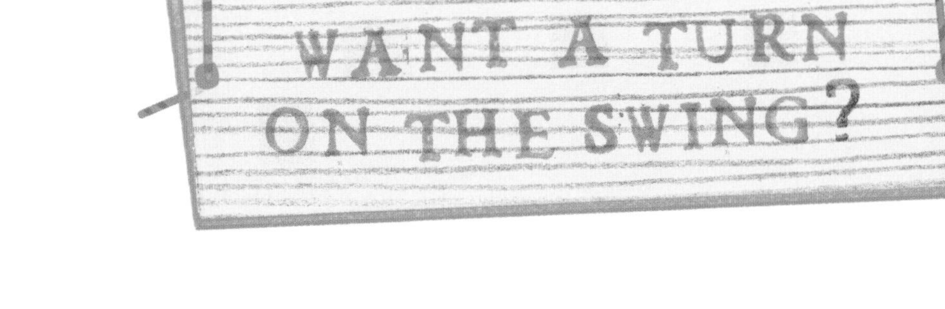

PAUL CRIED.

"I'VE MISSED SWINGING SO MUCH. I'VE MISSED YELLING ABOUT WHAT HAPPINESS IS!"

"A BIG ORANGE ORANGE!"

"MY MOTHER'S POTS AND
MY DAD'S HELICOPTER!"

"CARROT CAKE, GOLDFISH,
MARMALADE, AND TREES IN AUTUMN!"

"AN ORANGE BASKETBALL,
AND ROSE'S PET HAMSTER!"

welcome
to planet
Earth

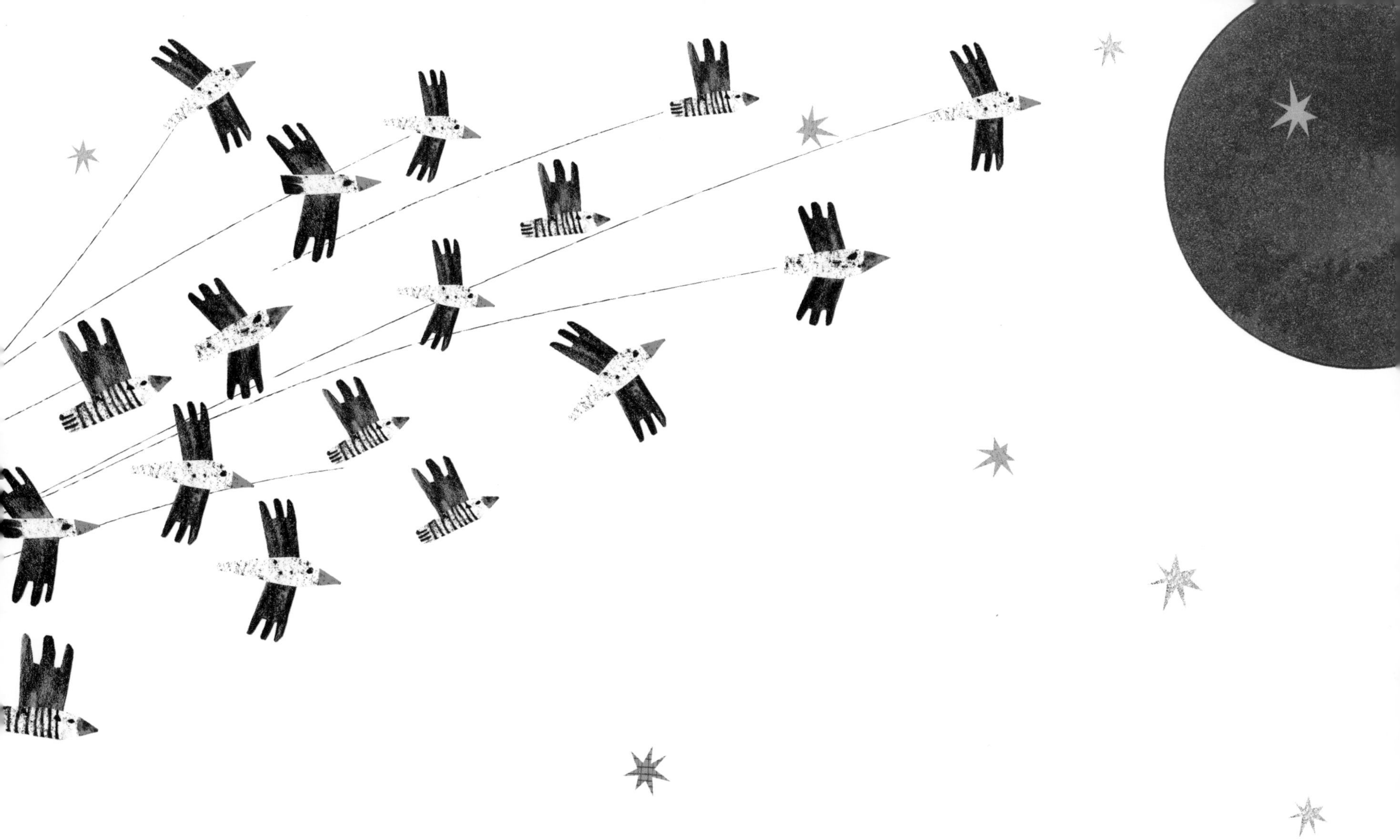

"BUT MOST OF ALL,

HAPPINESS IS A FOX!"

THE END

This is dedicated to everyone with whom I was, am and will be happy.

Aušra

To my teacher Jolanta, who once saw what I could not see in myself. To myself in the summer of 1981.
And for all little and not so little readers who are not afraid to make friends and feel love.

Evelina

Text by Evelina Daciūtė
Illustrations by Aušra Kiudulaitė

First published in the United Kingdom in 2018 by
Thames & Hudson Ltd, 181A High Holborn,
London WC1V 7QX

www.thamesandhudson.com

First published in the United States of America in 2018 by
Thames & Hudson Inc., 500 Fifth Avenue, New York, New York 10110

www.thamesandhudsonusa.com

British Library Cataloguing-in-Publication Data
A catalogue record for this book is available from the British Library

Library of Congress Control Number 2017958346

ISBN 978-0-500-65156-8

Printed and bound in China